QUACKER MEETS MRS. MOO
Tales from A Duck Named Quacker

THIS BOOK IS DEDICATED TO
ALL THE CHILDREN OF THE WORLD.

WRITTEN BY INSPIRATION FROM ABOVE,

ILLUSTRATED BY ORDERS FROM ABOVE,

PUBLISHED BY GRACE FROM ABOVE.

MAY THE GOOD LORD BLESS YOU ALL!

Ricky Van Shelton

SO QUACKER
THE DUCK
WENT ON HIS WAY...

...WAGGING HIS TAIL
LIKE A DOG.

AND HE DECIDED
TO REST
AT HIS FAVORITE SPOT...

BY THE POND,...

IN THE SHADE,
ON A LOG.

HE HAD JUST
CLOSED HIS EYES...

AND WAS ALMOST
ASLEEP,

WHEN ALL OF A
SUDDEN...

HE WAS KNOCKED
TO HIS FEET!

HE FLUTTERED AND
FLOPPED
AND HONKED AND QUACKED...

AND FLEW TO THE WOODS
BEFORE HE EVER
LOOKED BACK.

AND THERE BY THE
LOG
STOOD THE REASON HE FLEW.

IT WAS A COW
NAMED
MRS. MOO!

"QUACKER", SHE SAID
AS SHE CHEWED
ON SOME GRASS,

"I'M SORRY
I SCARED YOU,
BUT YOU SURE FLEW FAST!"

SO QUACKER
CAME WADDLING
BACK TO THE SHADE

TO REST,
AT LAST,
IN THE BED HE HAD MADE.

AND WHEN HE
WAS PERCHED
AND ALL SETTLED DOWN...

...HE SAID,
"MRS. MOO,
YOU SURE ARE A CLOWN...

...TO TAKE YOUR
LONG TAIL
AND KNOCK ME DOWN!"

THEN MRS. MOO SAID, "QUACKER, I DIDN'T SEE YOU THERE; FOR I WAS EATING MY LUNCH WITH MY HEAD IN THE AIR."

AND THE FLIES
AND MOSQUITOES
WERE BOTHERING ME...

...SO I TOOK MY
LONG TAIL
AND I SWATTED THREE!

"BUT WHEN MY
LONG TAIL
FLOPPED DOWN AGAIN...

IT HIT ON
YOUR HEAD,"
SHE SAID WITH A GRIN!

"AND ALTHOUGH
IT WAS FUNNY,
I DIDN'T MEAN TO;

BUT JUST
LIKE I SAID,
I NEVER SAW YOU."

FOR IT ISN'T NICE
TO SCARE SOMEONE
'CAUSE THEY MIGHT GET HURT
IF THEY START TO RUN.

AND IT NEVER
IS FUN
TO HURT ANYONE!